Finn and the Hiccups

For Fynn, Oscar, Sage, Olivia and Frances – MG

First published in 2008
by Wayland

This paperback edition published in 2009

Wayland
338 Euston Road
London NW1 3BH

Wayland Australia
Level 17/207 Kent Street
Sydney, NSW 2000

Series Editor: Louise John
Editor: Katie Powell
Cover design: Paul Cherrill
Design: D.R.ink
Consultant: Shirley Bickler

A CIP catalogue record for this book is available from the British Library.

ISBN 9780750254663 (hbk)
ISBN 9780750254670 (pbk)

Printed in China

Wayland is a division of Hachette Children's Books,
an Hachette Livre UK Company

www.hachettelivre.co.uk

Finn and
the Hiccups

Written by Mick Gowar
Illustrated by Tim Archbold

WAYLAND

Jim the Carter pulled on the reins.
The old horse stopped.

"Good morning, Finn," he said. "Why
are you standing in the middle of the
road, waving your arms about?"

"I need a lift," said Finn. "I'm off to seek my fortune."

"I'm off to Mayo to buy some potatoes," said Jim.

"Mayo's a great place to seek your fortune," said Finn and he climbed up on to the cart.

The road was long and boring.
"Tell me a story," said Jim.
"You're a great storyteller."
Finn thought for a minute.

"Did I ever tell you about the time
I played football with the King of
the Fairies?"

"We were playing against a team of giants. It was 56 goals each when the whistle blew. It was time for the penalty shoot-out..."

Finn's story was so funny, the miles slipped by and soon they were in Mayo.

"Will you come with me?" asked Jim.

"No," said Finn. "I feel a little tired.
I'll sit down on this mound and have
a little rest."

But, as Finn sat down, he heard a
voice coming from inside the mound.
"Can no one help us? Oh, can no
one help us?"

Finn leapt to his feet. There was
a little green trap door in the side
of the mound.

Finn lifted the little door.

A ladder led into the mound.
Finn began to climb down.

As he climbed, the voice got louder, "Can no one help us? Oh, can no one help us?"

A few steps from the bottom, Finn stopped and looked down. Below him were the king and queen of the fairies, sitting on golden thrones.

"Hic!" The queen leapt into the air.

A second later, "Hoc!" Up she
shot again.

"My poor queen!" said the king.
"Can no one help us?"

"Hac!" shouted the queen and leapt from her throne again.

"It's only hiccups," thought Finn.

"Hup!" yelled the queen.

"A fortune in fairy gold to anyone who can cure the queen!" cried the king.

"I know how to cure hiccups!"
thought Finn.

He jumped off the ladder.
"Yaaaargh — BOOOOH!" he bellowed.

"Guards!" yelled the king. "We're being attacked by a mortal!"

"It's all right!" Finn shouted.
"Look – I've cured the queen's hiccups!"

It was true. The queen sat quietly on her throne without a single "Hic!" "Hoc!" or "Hup!"

The king led Finn to a huge chest full
of fairy gold.

"Fill your pockets, mortal," said
the king.

So Finn filled his pockets, then with
a cheery farewell, he climbed back up
the ladder.

"Where have you been?" asked Jim.
"I've been waiting for hours!"

"I've been in the Land of the Fairies," said Finn. "I cured the queen's hiccups and now I'm rich – look!" He plunged his hands into his pockets and pulled out... dry leaves!

"They cheated me!" yelled Finn.

Jim laughed. "That was a great story," he said. "One of your best."

"But it's true," cried Finn.

"Of course it is," said Jim, with a wink.
"Of course it is."

START READING is a series of highly enjoyable books for beginner readers. **The books have been carefully graded to match the Book Bands widely used in schools.** This enables readers to be sure they choose books that match their own reading ability.

Look out for the Band colour on the book in our Start Reading logo.

The Bands are:

🔵	Pink Band 1
🔵	Red Band 2
🔵	Yellow Band 3
🔵	Blue Band 4
🔵	Green Band 5
🔵	Orange Band 6
🔵	Turquoise Band 7
🔵	Purple Band 8
🔵	Gold Band 9

START READING books can be read independently or shared with an adult. They promote the enjoyment of reading through satisfying stories supported by fun illustrations.

Mick Gowar has written more than 70 books for children, and likes to visit schools and libraries to give readings and lead workshops. He has also written plays and songs, and has worked with many orchestras. Mick writes his books in a shed in Cambridge.

Tim Archbold believes that making your fortune can be a difficult thing to do. Grumpy kings are hard to please, magic goats are always difficult to work with and the end of a rainbow is just over the next hill. But keep trying and have some fun on the way to your fortune...